Eddie's Ordeal

NEATE™ BOOK #4

by

Kelly Starling Lyons

FICTION

Published by Just Us Books
356 Glenwood Ave.
East Orange, NJ 07017
www.justusbooks.com

NEATE™ was created by Wade Hudson and is a trademark of
Just Us Books, Inc.

Cover art copyright 2004 by Peter Ambush.

EDDIE's ORDEAL

NEATE™ Book #4

ISBN: 978-0-940975-16-3

Library of Congress Cataloging-in-Publication Data is available

First edition Printed in Canada

10 9 8 7 6 5 4 3 2 1

For my heart, Patrick Alan Lyons; my treasure, Jordan Gabrielle Lyons;
and my heroine, Deborah Starling-Pollard.

Thanks,

Kelly

Eddie's Ordeal

NEATE™ BOOK #4

◆ CHAPTER ONE ◆

Doink, doink, doink. As the Monday afternoon sun began to fade, Eddie Delaney dribbled against the salted pavement of his driveway. Doink, doink. He shuffled the basketball over and over from his left hand, between his legs and then to his right. Doink. Eddie bounded toward the basket hanging over the garage for a lay-up. He tried jump shots from different angles, ran to the curb and sent the ball flying from his own version of three-point land. He missed as many shots as he landed.

Eddie wiped the sweat that trickled down from under his black skullcap with the sleeve of his yellow sweatshirt. An energetic warmth replaced the chill he felt when he first stepped out into the winter air. Eddie loved basketball but the skill didn't come easily. Now that he was a starter for the DuSable Junior High School Bulldogs, he had to work on his game every chance he got.

A familiar black Mercedes pulled up in front of Eddie's brick house. A tall, striking man wearing a heavy trench coat stepped out. Doink, doink.

"Hey Dad," Eddie yelled over his shoulder, without losing his rhythm.

"Looking good, son," Floyd Delaney said, standing to the side and watching for a bit.

Absorbed with practice, Eddie didn't see his father set his tan leather briefcase on their browning lawn. Mr. Delaney removed his coat and navy suit jacket, folded them neatly across the top of his case and rolled up the sleeves of his crisp Brooks Brothers shirt.

"Let your old man show you how it's done," he said.

Eddie turned to his father with an amused look. His dad never played ball in his work clothes. Eddie couldn't remember the last time they had played together at all.

"*You're* going to school *me*, the LeBron James of DuSable Junior High," Eddie ribbed, looking his dad up and down from his perfect faded haircut to his black wing-tip shoes. "This I've got to see."

Eddie tossed the ball to his dad. Standing across from each other, their differences were unmistakable. Mr. Delaney stood about a foot taller than Eddie. His smooth, coffee-colored face made some people guess at first that he was years younger. But his silver-sprinkled goatee, intense eyes and laugh lines that stayed invisible until he smiled revealed his more than five decades of life. Eddie, with his fresh face and happy-go-lucky spirit, didn't fool anyone. He looked exactly his age—13.

But the more someone looked at the pair, the more their similarities—deep dimples, rounded noses, long, slender fingers—became apparent too.

"Check," Mr. Delaney said, heaving the ball to his son.

"Check," Eddie answered and returned it to him.

Game faces replaced smiles. The challenge was on. Mr. Delaney faked to the right then made a drive from the left for the hoop. Eddie was quick and beat him to the goal. He threw up his hands to block his dad's shot. But he was no match for Mr. Delaney's height or skill. His father made the lay-up.

"Not too bad for an old man, huh?" Mr. Delaney crowed as they both huffed for breath.

"Not bad," Eddie said and tried to hide his grin.

Unsure what to say next, father and son just stood there in the driveway for an awkward moment. Seconds painfully dragged as their silence boomed louder than the whir of cars driving down the street.

"Well, I better get inside," Mr. Delaney said, finally. He picked up his briefcase and threw his coat and suit jacket over his arm. "You wrap it up soon too. I assume all of your homework is finished?"

"Yes, sir," Eddie said.

Doink, doink. With dusk painting the water-colored sky, Eddie jumped and aimed the ball toward the hoop. It nicked the rim and bounced on the pavement instead. Eddie smiled anyway. Ever since he had started doing better in school and in basketball, he and his dad had actually been getting along. Sure, his pops got on his nerves sometimes. They had clashed a lot in the past, but it was mostly over little things, like Eddie's room needing to be cleaned, stalling on completing his homework or not focusing in a certain class. If there was one thing Floyd Delaney, attorney-at-law, expected, it was achievement. Lately, though, Eddie felt closer to his dad.

But that was his secret. Eddie could never find the words to tell Mr. Delaney. As much as they loved each other, he and his dad never seemed to get over the distance that separated them. Even when they were near each other, something kept them apart.

The next morning at the corner of Mary and Washington Street, Eddie met the people who knew him better than anyone. Naimah Gordon, Elizabeth Butler, Anthony Young, and Tayesha Williams were there just like always. The five friends grew up together and lived on Mary Street within a few houses of each other. Their memories were stitched like a tapestry of friendship and silly feuds, laughter and tears, carefree summer days and the every-day dramas of growing up. They even had a name for their crew, NEATE, created from the first letter of each person's name.

Engaged in their own conversation, the girls walked ahead of Eddie and Anthony, who brought up the rear.

"I saw you and your dad outside yesterday," Anthony said as they turned from a residential block onto a commercial street.

"You did?" Eddie said. "Why didn't you stop by?"

"I didn't want to break up what you had going," Anthony said. "It was nice to see the two of you together."

"Yeah, can you believe it?" Eddie said with a lowered voice. "I can't believe the old man has game. He whipped me in wing tips. How crazy is that?"

Anthony pushed up his glasses and laughed.

"Don't worry, I'll keep it between you and me."

"Thanks man," Eddie said, laying a hand on his friend's shoulder. "I wouldn't want to let down my fans."

They chuckled again.

"What are you guys whispering about?" Naimah turned around and planted one of her hands playfully on her hip. "Hatching up some kind of conspiracy?"

"Maybe," Eddie said. "Why should you girls have a lock on secrets? You know we fellas have our classified information too."

Liz and Tayesha laughed.

At school, the friends hung out on the stone steps that led to DuSable's steel double front doors for a while before going inside. Students gathered in small clusters around them. The air clanged with chatter and the sound of buses pulling in.

"Hey Eddie," a cute girl with braids and large

almond eyes said as she walked by with her friends.

"Hey Mia," he said shyly to the Bulldogs cheerleader. They smiled at each other sweetly before she disappeared into the crowd.

"Hey Mia," Liz teased Eddie, imitating his sugary voice. Eddie turned around to see who was mocking him. Liz tried to look innocent and then started cracking up.

"That's alright, girlfriend," Eddie said, using Liz's favorite nickname. "There's plenty of me to go around." Eddie was always quick with a come back. He and Liz ragged on each other like brother and sister.

"Whatever," Liz said with a laugh and a roll of her eyes.

The school day went quickly, but by last period, Eddie couldn't wait for the bell to ring. As minutes ticked toward dismissal, he tapped his Nike sneaker anxiously against the hardwood floor. "What is taking so long?" he thought and leaned his cheek against his fist. Eddie wanted to hit the court.

He could still remember how it felt when he made the winning basket a few weeks before in the opening game of the season. The pats from the team. The cheers from his classmates. The pride on his dad's face. He could get used to that.

Eddie watched Mrs. Smith, who was also his homeroom teacher, sort through a stack of envelopes. She stood up, walked down the rows of desks and handed an envelope to each student. When Eddie got his, he knew just what it was: mid-semester progress reports. Ugh! Eddie peeled the envelope open and scanned the grades for each of his classes. Whew, he thought, leaning back in his seat and cheesing as he took in his marks. Not bad. Then, he saw it. The one thing that could wreck his day—make that his life. An ugly, digitized D in language arts. D for disaster. He sat forward with his mouth hanging open in disbelief. He just kept staring at the D in shock.

"Eddie, Eddie," Liz called from the next row. "How did you do?"

"Alright," he said and stuffed the sheet in his Lakers backpack without looking her way. Just then the bell rang and let him off the hook. "I gotta go."

As Eddie rushed into the crowd of classmates, Liz followed him with her eyes.

"What's up with Eddie?" Liz asked Naimah as she walked out the door.

Naimah shrugged. "He's probably just trying to get to practice," she said. "You know how much that boy loves basketball."

On the way to the locker room, Eddie kept thinking about what his dad would say. A D was bad news with most parents. But for Floyd Delaney, now a civil rights attorney and community activist, it was inexcusable. He could already hear the lecture and his dad's frustrated tone: "Eddie, I expected more from you." To lay on the guilt, he might even call Eddie by his full name, Martin Edward, invoking his famous namesake Dr. Martin Luther King, Jr.

Eddie's head ached already.

Instead of cracking jokes in the locker room as usual, Eddie headed right for the basketball court. From the beginning, his game was off. Eddie ran toward the hoop for a lay-up during a shooting drill. The ball bounced off the rim and onto the floor. He waited his turn and tried a three-pointer next. It was an air ball.

Eddie passed the ball across the court to his teammate. They tossed it back and forth to each other. But Eddie's thoughts were as far away as the moon on a gloomy night.

"What's the matter, Delaney?" Coach

Hamilton asked him after practice.

"Nothing Coach, just having a bad day," Eddie said. "I'll get it together."

"You better," the Coach teased him and patted his shoulder. "We play Carver in two weeks."

During the walk home, Eddie kept wondering what he would do about his bad grade, what he would say to his folks. By the time he got to his tree-shaded block on Mary Street, Eddie decided he would just get it over with. He brushed aside the worrying for a second. Progress reports didn't count, he easily convinced himself. They were just notices to let parents know how their kids were doing so far. Why keep stressing about it? Eddie would give his dad the grades and tell him that he'd do better by report card time. His father would let him have it for a while but then things would be okay.

Relieved, Eddie unlocked the front door of his home and stepped into a sunny hallway lined with paintings. Vibrant scenes of Black culture sprang to life —a bride and groom jumping the broom, a grandfather teaching his grandson to cast a fishing rod, an infant tucked under a patchwork quilt. His mother's art always let him know that he was home—that and her cooking. The smell of her pot roast and cornbread made his stomach grumble.

"Mom, I'm home," Eddie announced. He tugged off his skullcap and gloves, and walked to the living room to bask in the warmth of its glowing fireplace.

"Hey babe," Juanita Delaney greeted him from the kitchen. She walked into their living room, which was decorated with sculptures and furniture accented in African fabric, and gave him a hug. "How was your day?"

"Okay," he said, sounding distracted. "I need to talk to dad. Is he upstairs?"

"He's in his office," his mother answered.

Eddie walked across the maple hardwood to the French doors and saw his father's head bent over a mega-sized law text.

"Dad, can I talk to you for a minute?" Eddie stood in the doorway and asked.

Mr. Delaney looked up from his book.

"Sure son, what's up?"

Eddie sat down in a mahogany chair opposite his father. He took in his dad's neatly groomed mustache. He looked at his father's massive hands, and at his own that seemed so puny by comparison. He always felt so small next to him.

Eddie gazed at his father's shelves bursting with important books and the wall with his framed degrees and awards: Magna cum laude from Shaw University. Top honors in his law school class. Mason and fraternity certificates. Eddie started feeling anxious all over again. He knew how much his dad cared about grades. But it was just one class. He could pull it up. Eddie hoped his dad would understand.

"I got my progress report," Eddie said and broke the silence. "It's mostly pretty good."

"Mostly?" Mr. Delaney caught on and stuck out his hand. "Let me see."

His father glanced down at the grades and nodded. Suddenly, his eyes grew large and he stared at Eddie.

"Martin Edward, I know that's not a D in language arts. Has your mother seen this?"

"No sir, I wanted to show you first," Eddie said. He looked down at his shuffling feet.

"Didn't you get a B last time?" Mr. Delaney asked. "What happened?"

"I don't know," Eddie said. "I've been working hard. I guess not as hard as I thought."

"I guess not," Mr. Delaney said, scowling. "Maybe you've been working hard on the wrong things. Is that all you have to say?"

"I can bring it up," Eddie offered quickly. "I'll talk to Mr. Nelson tomorrow and study really hard and raise the grade by the time report cards come out. I still have time."

"Eddie, we had a deal," Mr. Delaney said. "You could play on the basketball team as long as you kept up your marks. Go on and get ready for dinner while your mother and I talk about what we're going to do."

As he trudged up the stairs, Eddie realized that he hadn't thought about the team. His dad couldn't take that away from him. Could he?

At dinner, Eddie and his parents ate for a while without speaking. The clank of silverware was the only break from the crushing silence. Then, his dad said the unthinkable.

"Eddie," Mr. Delaney began. "Your mom and I hate to do this. But we're going to have to pull you off the team."

"No, not that," Eddie said as he looked from one parent to the other. "Dad, Mom, come on, I'll do better, I promise. Just please don't make me quit. I'm finally getting a chance to start.

The Bulldogs need me."

"I'm sorry, honey," Mrs. Delaney said. "We know how much this means to you. But grades come first. We talked about that from the beginning."

"Fine, whatever," Eddie mumbled as his eyes started to burn. Defeated, he slumped in his seat.

"What did you say?" Mr. Delaney asked him sharply.

"Nothing," Eddie said while he gazed down at the floor. Suddenly, his appetite disappeared. "May I be excused?"

"Yes, I think you'd better," Mr. Delaney said.

"I don't know what's wrong with that boy," Eddie heard his dad say to his mom as he climbed the stairs.

Eddie shut his room door and sat on the edge of his bed. He sank his face in his palms. He couldn't believe this was really happening.

Didn't his dad understand anything?

◆ CHAPTER TWO ◆

The next morning, Eddie woke up in purple darkness. He rolled over and peeked at his alarm clock with one sleepy eye. In red digits, the time 6:00 called him to action. Eddie crawled out of bed and headed for the bathroom. He splashed water on his face and gazed at his mocha-colored reflection in the mirror. A handsome boy with a fuzz of hair and puffy, ringed eyes stared back. Eddie looked beat but he didn't care. He pulled on some blue sweats, sneakers, a striped scarf, grabbed his basketball and quietly descended the stairs for the driveway. Ever since Bulldogs' practice started, he had been getting up extra early to work on his game.

Outside, the icy wind caught Eddie's breath and chilled his hands. He rubbed his palms together and breathed white puffs into the early morning air. Eddie dribbled and aimed for the hoop. His hand stayed poised like an NBA baller's as the sphere sailed through the air. Swoosh. The ball caught nothing but net.

"And the crowd goes wild," he said, cupping

his palms to his mouth and imitating the cheers that roared in his mind.

Eddie dribbled some more and focused again. He bent his knees, extended his right arm upward and popped his wrist. The ball sailed through the air, circled the hoop then veered off without going in. Frustrated by the easy miss, Eddie didn't see Anthony ride up his bike.

"Hey Eddie," the slight boy called out. He pulled over for a minute and sat his bulging sack of newspapers down. "How's it going?"

"Not good," Eddie said, between dribbles. "I got a D in language arts and my pops took me off the team."

"For real?" Anthony said, wincing and squinting behind his wire-rimmed glasses. "A D? That's rough. What are you going to do?"

"I don't know what I can do," Eddie said and let the ball fly again.

"Once Floyd Delaney's mind is made up, that's it."

"Keep your head up," Anthony said. "We'll think of something. We'll talk about it on the way to school. See you later."

Back on his bike, Anthony rode down the

street and tossed papers as he went.

Eddie bounced the ball and concentrated again on the net. Just when he began to shoot, a loud noise startled him and made him miss the hoop. The ball landed in the hedges and rolled onto the grass. His father had let the door slam behind him as he walked outside

"Eddie, if you want to get up so early, you can work on language arts," Mr. Delaney bellowed from the doorway. "Basketball is the least of your worries right now."

"Yes sir," Eddie answered with military precision.

He sighed, collected the ball, tucked it under his arm and headed back inside. It was just going to be one of those days.

At 7:40 a.m., Eddie met his friends near the corner and they walked to DuSable Junior High School together.

"What was up with you yesterday?" Liz asked Eddie. "You were acting weird."

"I'm sorry," he said. "I was just out of it. You'll all find out anyway so I might as well tell you now. Mr. Nelson gave me a D."

"Noooo," Liz said. "What did your parents say?"

"What do you think?" Eddie asked her. "They flipped. I'm off the Bulldogs."

"Really?" Liz asked.

"I'm so sorry, Eddie," Tayesha chimed in. "I know how much playing ball means to you."

"Thanks," Eddie said. "I don't know how I'm supposed to tell Coach and the guys."

"Did you try bargaining with your dad?" Anthony asked. "Like, promise to work really hard to bring your grades up and ask for another chance?"

"Annnk," Eddie said, mimicking the sound of a buzzer. "Tried that. No deal."

"What about working on your mom?" Liz asked. "Can you get her on your side and then ask her to talk to your dad?"

"Try again," Eddie said. "She's not hearing me either. It's just hopeless."

The friends walked the rest of the way to school in silence. It was hard trying to figure out what to do.

"I have to talk to Coach before the bell," Eddie said when they arrived at DuSable. "Catch you later."

As Eddie hurried off, Liz watched him until he

disappeared down the corridor.

"How are we going to help Eddie?" Liz finally asked her friends. "We need a plan."

"We can have a meeting at my house," Naimah offered. As president of the student council, she was always designing strategies. "There has to be something we can do."

In the locker room, Eddie broke the news to Coach Hamilton.

"How did this happen, Eddie?" the coach asked him.

"I don't know," Eddie said as he shook his head. "I've been getting up early to practice. I guess I've been slacking on Mr. Nelson's stuff. But I can turn it around. I can do better. I just need another chance. My dad just doesn't want to listen."

"I can't say that I blame him," Coach Hamilton said. "You're here to learn. Basketball is a privilege."

"I know," Eddie said, "and I understand that. I just wish my dad believed in me. All I need is another chance." He said nothing for a while and just looked at his coach. Then Eddie tried a long shot.

"Do you think you could talk to him?"

"Delaney, I know you want all of this to go away," Coach Hamilton said. "But you got yourself into it. It's up to you to get yourself out. I can't talk to your dad. You're his son and it's his call. We'll miss you on the team. But there's nothing I can do. It's up to you to show and prove."

"Okay Coach," Eddie said, softly. "I'm sorry I let you down."

Eddie moped out of the gym and walked slowly through the rushing students toward his homeroom.

"Watch it," a female voice said sharply.

"Sorry," Eddie mumbled. Just what he needed—attitude. He turned to look at whom he had bumped into. When he saw that it was Mia Walker, he perked up a little.

"Hey Mia," Eddie said. "Are you okay?"

"Yeah," she said. "I didn't know that was you. How's it going?"

"I'm cool," he said. "How are you?"

"Okay," she said and smiled. "Well, I guess we both better hurry before we get to homeroom late."

"Yeah, we better. See you," Eddie said and began to walk away.

"Hey Eddie," Mia called as she walked away from him backwards.

Eddie turned around.

"See you at the game," she said grinning.

Eddie faked a smile for Mia. But as soon as he turned around, he frowned.

Eddie made it to homeroom just before the bell. Naimah was first to notice the petite, brown-skinned girl standing next to Mrs. Smith.

"Who's that?" she mouthed to Liz, who sat across from her.

Liz shrugged her shoulders.

"Everyone, this is Jasmine King," Mrs. Smith said a few moments later as she introduced the new girl to the class.

"Her family moved here from Norfolk, Virginia," she said. "Let's make her feel at home."

"Jasmine, you can take that open seat," Mrs. Smith said and pointed to an empty desk near Liz.

Right away, Liz noticed Jasmine's sleek chin-length bob, red glittery sweater and button-front black mini.

"Girlfriend, your outfit is tight," she whispered.

"Thanks," Jasmine said, eyeing Liz's long-sleeved denim dress, star choker and striped tights. Her chestnut-colored hair was twisted in the front with the rest in shoulder-grazing curls. "I like your style too," Jasmine complimented.

At the end of homeroom, the students gathered their belongings and headed out the door.

"Liz, Jasmine," Mrs. Smith called them to her desk.

"I noticed the two of you have some of the same classes," she said. "Liz, could you show Jasmine around?"

"Sure," Liz said.

The girls walked down the hallway together.

"So what's Norfolk like?" Liz asked as they navigated through the busy hallway.

"Actually I haven't lived there long enough to really know," Jasmine said. "The only place I really call home is Pittsburgh, Pennsylvania, where I was born and spend time with my grandparents every summer. My dad is in the Navy. We've lived all over—Jacksonville, San Diego, Hawaii. Norfolk was just our last stop."

"Hawaii?" Liz said. "Wow, that's cool. I know

you miss that weather now. But all that moving around must be hard."

"Sometimes," Jasmine said. "You get used to it. The worst part is making new friends."

"Well, you've got one now."

Jasmine smiled.

"What's going on over there?" Jasmine asked Liz.

Liz saw a small crowd gathered around the school bulletin board. She and Jasmine lined up for their chance to see the pink flyer that had the attention of dozens of their peers. The paper announced auditions for the school talent show.

"Oh cool," Jasmine said. "A talent show!"

"You perform?" Liz said. "Me too. What are you into?"

"I sing," Jasmine replied.

"No way," Liz said. "Singing is my life."

The girls grinned at each other as they hustled to make science class before the bell. They seemed destined to be friends.

◆ CHAPTER THREE ◆

After school, Eddie, Liz, Tayesha, Anthony and Naimah walked home together. Usually Eddie entertained them with funny observations about the day. Or he would tease Liz and ham it up with the others, but today he was quiet all the way to Mary Street. When the friends stopped to chat before going their separate ways, Eddie made tracks.

"I'm on lockdown," Eddie said. "I'll see y'all around."

"Poor Eddie," Naimah said when he left. "He's really got it bad. Are we still meeting at my house?"

"You know I'm there, girlfriend," Liz said.

"So are we," Tayesha and Anthony said together.

"How about 4 p.m.?" Naimah asked. "I'll have the snacks ready. Try to bring some ideas with you. We've figured out tough things before. We can handle this one too."

Anthony traveled down the block toward the

townhouse he shared with his mom. His mother, Pat Young, was working from home. As advertising sales manager for the *Daily World*, a local newspaper, she had more freedom with her schedule than most mothers. She gave him a hug when he walked in.

"How was school?" Ms. Young asked her only child.

"Okay for me," Anthony said. "Eddie's not doing too hot."

"No? What's wrong?"

"He's been practicing so hard for the Bulldogs that he let his grade slip in Mr. Nelson's class," he said. "He got a D on his progress report and Mr. and Mrs. Delaney took him off the team."

"That's too bad," Ms. Young said. "But maybe if he does better, they'll give him another chance."

"Maybe," said Anthony. He was raised by his mom and always admired the relationship between Eddie and his dad. "Eddie knows his dad really cares about him. He tried to impress Mr. Delaney by raising his game. Now, he has to give up the team. Sometimes Mr. Delaney just expects so much from him."

Ms. Young said nothing for a while and seemed

to be pondering something.

"I see what you mean," she said. "I know it feels really hard to be a kid sometimes. But it's hard being a parent too."

Anthony thought about what his mom said as he got ready for the meeting. Eddie's folks made him quit the team. He felt like everyone was against him. But Anthony had seen how proud Mr. Delaney was of Eddie and the way they bonded when they played ball. It made sense. Mr. Delaney was probably hurting too.

At Naimah's house, Liz was the first to show up.

"Hey girlfriend," she said warmly when Naimah answered the door and gave her a hug. They went to the comfy kitchen, their favorite meeting place, where Naimah had tortilla chips and salsa, fruit punch and cookies set up on the island. A picture window framed by red gingham curtains looked out onto the backyard. The wood-paneled walls gave the space a country feel.

"You changed," Naimah said when she noticed Liz's new outfit. "Always the diva."

"Thanks. You like?" Liz said, spinning around supermodel-style to show off her new black V-neck sweater, black-and-white striped flared jeans and coordinated boots. She loved to style almost as much as she loved to sing.

"My dad surprised me with the outfit for winning that karaoke contest last week."

She hopped onto a bar stool next to her friend. Naimah's little brother Rodney tiptoed to the doorway into the kitchen and tried to listen in. Liz saw his shadow.

"I think we have company," she whispered to Naimah and pointed in Rodney's direction.

"So what's new with you?" Liz said loudly as Naimah sneaked toward her brother on the checkered tile. "Anything juicy to share?"

"Yeah," Naimah said as she crept. "Did I tell you about. . ."

"Looking for something?" Naimah shouted suddenly. Her unexpected movement startled Rodney. He jumped and scampered away.

"What a pest," Naimah said and laughed. "He's always into everything I do."

"He just wuvs you," Liz said while batting her eyes. They giggled until their sides ached.

"So what do you think of the new girl?" Naimah asked.

"She seems real cool," Liz said as she reached

for a handful of chips. "Turns out she's a singer like me. We're both going to try out for the talent show."

"We should invite her to hang out with us one day," Naimah said.

The doorbell rang and interrupted their conversation. It was Tayesha. Anthony showed up next. It was 4:10 p.m. and everyone was there. The friends started the meeting by munching on chips and talking about Eddie.

Naimah, who always fell into the role of leader, got things moving.

"So, any suggestions?" she asked.

"We could help Eddie with his language arts homework," Tayesha suggested. "Look over his essays, take turns studying with him."

"Great idea," Naimah said. "Anything else?"

"We could help him think of ways to prove to his father that he deserves another chance," Liz said. "Maybe Eddie could do extra credit in Mr. Nelson's class, come right home and hit the books. You know, butter Mr. Delaney up."

"Right, right," Naimah said and nodded. "What about you, Anthony? Any thoughts?"

"I'm just wondering why Mr. Delaney is so

tough," he said. "Sometimes he seems to drive Eddie really hard."

"I don't know," Naimah said. "But that's a good question. Maybe we should snoop around and see what we can find out. I think we can also support Eddie by treating him just like we usually do. We don't want him to feel that we pity him or anything. Eddie's too proud for that."

•••••

Down the block, Eddie laid in bed reading *Monster* by Walter Dean Myers. It was the next book on his class list. His mom knocked on his open bedroom door.

"How about a peace offering?" she said, smiling and holding a bowl of popcorn.

In spite of himself, Eddie grinned. "Thanks Mom."

"I know you think we're just being hard on you," Mrs. Delaney said as she sat next to him on his twin bed. "But we're doing this because we love you. Life isn't going to give you a break."

"I know I messed up," Eddie said and tried to appeal to his mom. "But everybody makes mistakes. Don't I deserve another chance?"

"Prove to your father and me that you're

serious and we'll see," his mom said. "That's the best I can do."

Mrs. Delaney walked out of the room and up the stairs to her cluttered attic studio. Unfinished pieces sat on easels. Tubes of paint rested on the floor and on tables. She had an art show coming up. Like legendary painter Jacob Lawrence, Mrs. Delaney was inspired by Black history. She also loved capturing the simple, touching moments of Black life in her work.

Her work-in-progress was a series that showcased the strength of Black women from Africa through slavery to the present. Mrs. Delaney pushed strands of skinny braids from over her eyes to behind her ear, dipped a brush into her palette of vivid colors and began to create.

A while later, Mr. Delaney came home with his briefcase in one hand and a couple sacks of Chinese food in the other.

"Dinner is served," he hollered on his way to the kitchen. "Come and get it!"

Eddie plodded down the stairs. He wasn't looking forward to facing his dad. When they saw each other, father and son mumbled a greeting and made their plates without speaking. They sat down at the table and ate in silence. Though he kept his eyes locked on his food, Eddie could feel his dad looking at him. Was it just him, or was his mom's collection of gospel choir figurines staring at him too?

"How's that homework coming?" Mr. Delaney asked him finally.

"Fine," Eddie answered, without looking up. The quicker he finished eating, he thought to himself, the sooner he could get out of there.

Brriinngg. The phone gave Mr. Delaney a way out of the uncomfortable situation.

"Hello," he answered.

"Hey honey," he said after a short pause.

It was Eddie's big sister Daisey calling from Spelman College. She made the Dean's List every semester and seemed to always do the right thing. Like Eddie, she was named after a courageous civil rights icon—Daisy Bates. Back in the 1950s, Bates had helped to coordinate the effort to integrate public schools in Little Rock, Arkansas.

Mr. Delaney smiled at something his daughter said.

"Here Juanita," he said and gave Eddie's mom the phone when she walked in. "Daisey wants to tell you something."

"Now, your sister has the right idea," Mr. Delaney said when he returned to the table. "She has just been elected treasurer of the student government."

"Good for her," Eddie said.

Then he mumbled something to himself: "I'm not Daisey. I'm me."

◆ CHAPTER FOUR ◆

The days sped by and soon it was Thursday, time for talent show auditions. Liz had gotten to know Jasmine even better. They had a lot in common—a love of clothes, and a passion for singing. They even went crazy for the same legends—Stevie Wonder, Marvin Gaye, Phyllis Hyman, Roberta Flack and Donny Hathaway. Many kids didn't even know who some of those singers were. After school, Liz and Jasmine waited with the other talent show hopefuls in the auditorium. Neither girl knew what the other was singing. Liz and Jasmine had agreed to keep it secret so they wouldn't be tempted into a catty competition.

Liz went first, crooning "Fallin'" by Alicia Keys. Her hair was done up in long, patterned cornrows that would have done the singer proud. Liz smiled as she got into the groove of the song and watched people in the audience sing along. Everyone was loving her. They began clapping before she even finished.

"Liz, you were soooo good," Jasmine raved

when Liz came back to her seat.

"Girl, you've got skills."

"Thanks girlfriend," Liz said and sat back in her seat with a satisfied smile. "You're going to wow 'em too."

The friends watched a dance number and a monologue. Now, it was Jasmine's turn.

She stood and walked up the steps to the stage. Jasmine seemed to transform into someone else as she positioned herself behind the microphone and waited for the notes of her old-school classic to start. As the first notes of Mariah Carey's "Hero" filled the open space, Jasmine closed her eyes and let the music take her away.

She hit every riff, every high note. Like the rest of the people there, Liz was moved to silence. Goose pimples crept up her arm. She couldn't believe what she was hearing. Usually, Liz was the one who blew out the competition. At the end of the song, Jasmine's voice just lingered—a perfect ending. Everyone sat still for a moment, then jumped to their feet. Liz stood up and applauded, too. But why did she feel so funny?

It wasn't that she was hatin' on Jasmine. But Liz had always been the star of DuSable Junior High. She didn't expect Jasmine to sound *that* good. When Jasmine came back, Liz hugged her new friend and congratulated her on the audition. She meant every word of praise but she had a creepy feeling nagging at her too.

After school, NEATE started "Operation Eddie." Anthony had the first shift. He went home with Eddie so they could study for a test the next day. At 3:30 p.m., they sat at the glass-topped kitchen table and quizzed each other.

"Hey Anthony," Mrs. Delaney greeted her son's friend when she walked in the room.

"How's your mom?"

"She's doing well," he said.

"You all have everything you need?" Mrs. Delaney asked, pouring herself some cranberry juice.

"Yes ma'am," they answered. A crumpled bag of barbecue chips sat nearby as proof.

"Well, I'll let you boys get back to it," she said, grinning.

Eddie and Anthony were deep in study mode when they heard a key turning and then the sound of the front door opening.

"Oh great," Eddie said. "He's home early."

Eddie tried to ignore the sound of his dad's

heavy footsteps. But he knew the routine. His father would hang up his trench on the coat tree, drop his briefcase in his office, then make his way to the kitchen. Sure enough, a few minutes later, Mr. Delaney walked into the room where the two boys were studying.

"Hey there, Anthony," Mr. Delaney said as he strolled to the stainless steel refrigerator to fix himself a snack. "I didn't know you were here. How's the studying going?"

"Pretty good," Anthony answered. He brightened when he saw Mr. Delaney. "I think we're almost ready for the test tomorrow."

"Thanks for studying with Eddie," Mr. Delaney said. "You're a good friend and a bright student. You remind me of Daisey."

"You can learn something from your buddy," Mr. Delaney said to Eddie, before leaving the room. Eddie kept his eyes glued to his book. As soon as his father was gone, he rolled his eyes.

Anthony watched but didn't say anything at first.

"You're really lucky," he said, suddenly.

"Lucky?" Eddie said and looked up at him. "Are you kidding? I have the worse luck in the world. I'm off the Bulldogs. I'm struggling to get my grades together. I'm basically on house arrest."

"I mean to have a dad like Mr. Delaney," Anthony said.

"You like him?" Eddie said. "You can have him."

"I hear you," Anthony said. "But think about the deal with me and my dad. I thought he was dead all those years, then found out he was alive. We're writing letters to get to know each other. But you have a dad right here with you. And he's been here all the time. I wish I had that."

Eddie said nothing and kept studying. But secretly he began to ponder what his friend said.

Friday, after homeroom, Jasmine and Liz checked the list of chosen ones who made the talent show. They scanned down the roster. There they were: Elizabeth Butler, and a few names down, Jasmine King. Both of them made it. The girls hugged each other and jumped up and down.

"Now, we can practice together," Jasmine said.

"You know it," Liz replied. She couldn't believe she'd had a moment of envy. Jasmine was so cool.

As they walked for Spanish class, they passed a few classmates who had tried out too.

"Hey Jasmine," Kyanna Hayes called out. "Did you make it?"

"Yeah girl," Jasmine said with a grin. "Did you?"

Kyanna held both thumbs high. "I'll see you at practice."

"You can really sing," Kyle Edwards complimented Jasmine.

Liz got sloppy seconds. People tossed her a quick hi after gushing over Jasmine. What was she—the tacky shirt that no one wanted, even when it made the clearance rack?

At lunchtime, Liz, Jasmine and Naimah got in line. They plopped pizza and orange drink on their trays, but passed on the slimy-looking rice pudding. As they walked toward their table, Jasmine stalled and looked awkward.

"What's wrong?" Liz asked her.

"Kyanna and April already asked me to sit with them," Jasmine said. "I want to sit with you, but I don't know what to do."

"Go on, girlfriend," Liz said. "It's no biggie. I'll catch you later."

"Are you sure?" Jasmine asked. Liz nodded.

"Okay, I'll see you after school, right? For

practice?"

"Of course," Liz said.

Jasmine said goodbye and walked over to the table where Kyanna and the others were waiting.

Liz grinned, but inside she steamed. Liz Butler taking a backseat to someone. Unh unh. She didn't know what to think. When she and Naimah reached the table by the window that NEATE had claimed when they became eighth graders, they saw that their friends were already there.

"Where's Jasmine?" Tayesha asked.

"She's over there, eating with her *friends*," Liz said, with more bite than she meant.

"Ouch," Eddie said and grimaced. "I felt that over here."

"Eddie," Naimah said as she gave him a look that said, 'Not now.'

"I heard you made the talent show," Anthony said to change the subject. "Congratulations. As if there was any doubt."

"Yeah, girl, you know you can sing better than anyone," Tayesha said. "We know who's going to win."

Liz smiled but she wasn't so sure anymore.

◆ CHAPTER FIVE ◆

Two weeks had gone by since Eddie quit the Bulldogs and he was struggling with mixed feelings too. He had already missed a few minor games. He tried to forget about the upcoming match against DuSable's chief rival: Carver Middle School. Eddie didn't want to go. He couldn't be there on the court with his teammates or even on the bench, so why would he put himself through the drama of watching them play from the stands? It wasn't even worth it.

At his friends' urging, Eddie finally gave in. He agreed to ask his parents if he could attend. He was going to have to deal with being off the Bulldogs at some point. Might as well be now. To his surprise, his mom and dad said yes. On game day, Liz, Tayesha, Anthony, Naimah and Eddie walked into the packed gym together. They sat in the middle of the eager crowd.

"There they are," Liz said, raising her voice to compete with the clamor around them. She pointed to the guys from Carver's squad. "It's a shame they came all this way to lose."

Even Eddie had to laugh at that. It had been a long time since he had sat on those wooden bleachers. Before he got a chance to be a starting guard for the Bulldogs, Eddie had warmed the bench. But at least he was still part of the team. Sitting amidst his classmates, he was just like everybody else: a bystander. At first, Eddie moped. Then the energy got him. He rooted for his teammates, jeered when the other team scored and danced in his seat when the step team performed. He gobbled goodies from the concession stand at half-time. But as the action picked up, Eddie got antsy. It felt weird being on the other side. As he watched the Bulldogs score without him, the camaraderie of the guys and the between-game chatter, he started getting depressed. He spotted Mia on the floor with the other cheerleaders. At the same time she saw him, sitting on the bleachers in his street clothes.

She gave Eddie a confused look and shrugged her pompoms as if to ask what was going on. Eddie just looked away.

•••••

With the house to themselves, Eddie's parents enjoyed a quiet moment together. They sat beside each other on the chocolate colored leather couch and listened to the smooth sounds of the Isley

Brothers. Mr. Delaney stood up and extended his hand. Mrs. Delaney grinned and allowed him to help her up. They two-stepped in the living room as if they were out on a date. When the CD player switched to another track, they slid back onto the couch and Mrs. Delaney started talking.

"So what do you want to do about Eddie?" she asked her husband as she cuddled next to him. "The two of you can't keep walking around here like strangers."

Mr. Delaney frowned. "I know," he said. "But he has to learn that grades come first. What would have happened if we let things slide when we were his age?"

"That was another time, Floyd," Mrs. Delaney said. "Another era. Things have changed. Kids nowadays don't face the same pressures that we did. And I remember a certain young man who made a few mistakes in his day."

"What mistake are you talking about, Juanita?" Mr. Delaney said as he pulled away and grew tense.

"Why are you getting so defensive? You know that I would never go there," his wife said softly.

Her words did little to soothe Mr. Delaney. Her

mention of a mistake from his past had him on edge.

"You think it's so different now, Juanita," he said."Look at the statistics. Pick up any newspaper and you'll read about how people think young Black men are more likely to end up in prison than in college, about the racism some young Black men face in the workplace. I just want him to be prepared."

"Eddie's a good kid," she said. "We've raised him well."

"I know that," Mr. Delaney said. "But I want him to understand the legacy he comes from. He has the opportunities he does because people struggled, died, to give him that break. Wasting those chances, squandering his gifts, is like throwing away their work—our work—like everything we did means nothing."

"I hear you and I understand," Mrs. Delaney said. "Remember, I was there with you. But we have to find a balance. Eddie needs standards, yes, but he needs a dad who can be a friend, too."

◆ CHAPTER SIX ◆

In the days following the game, Eddie's spirit seemed to wilt. He walked with his head down. He ate his lunch in silence. He even snapped at his friends a few times. His buddies forgave him and rallied to keep him going. Tayesha, his next study partner, dropped by his house so they could work on their essays for Language Arts. The rest of NEATE got busy on phase two of their plan.

One evening after dinner, Naimah asked her mother what she knew about Mr. Delaney.

"Mom, do you know what Mr. Delaney did before he was a lawyer?" she asked innocently.

"No, not really. I know he has always been interested in law," she said. "I think I heard something about him helping to coordinate campaigns for Black political candidates when he was younger. But I'm not sure. Why?"

"Just curious," Naimah said, cagily. "I'm working on a class project and was considering interviewing him."

"Oh, that's nice Nai," she said. "Why don't you just give him a call and ask him? I'm sure he'd be happy to spare some time."

If only it were that easy, Naimah thought.

A few houses down, Anthony started working on his mom too.

"Mom, isn't Mr. Delaney from the South?" he asked her.

"Yeah, I think so," Ms. Young said. "Somewhere in North Carolina."

"Do you know what part?"

"I think Raleigh. Why all the questions?" Ms. Young asked her son, who thought he was being slick. Then, she caught on. "Anthony Young, what are you up to?"

"Nothing," he said.

"Anthony?" she asked him again, her voice rising into a you-can't-fool-your-mama tone.

Anthony knew he was busted. He broke and it all came out in a rush.

"We're trying to help Eddie and his dad make up and we wondered if there's some reason why Mr. Delaney acts so hard sometimes so we're trying to learn more about his past to see if there's something we can find out that will help," he said, panting at the end.

"Whoa, slow down," Ms. Young said. "Have a

seat. Now, what are you doing?"

Anthony sank into the cushioned couch and looked at his mom. He knew she wouldn't rat them out. What did he have to lose?

"We're trying to find out more about Mr. Delaney's background," Anthony said. "Maybe there's some reason why he's so tough on Eddie. Maybe we can find out something that will help Eddie understand where his dad is coming from."

"I know you want to help Anthony," Ms. Young said. "But it sounds like you're dipping into something that's not your business."

"I know, Mom," he said. "But we gotta do something. We can tell Eddie is hurting. Mr. Delaney probably is too. Can you help us out? Maybe check out the newspaper archives?"

Ms. Young looked at the sincerity in her son's face. Anthony widened his eyes behind his glasses to appear extra humble. How could she turn him down?

"I can't promise anything," she said. "But I'll see what I can find."

Anthony jumped up and hugged his mother.

"You know you're alright," he said, nearly knocking her over. "For a mom, that is."

"Gee thanks," Ms. Young said, laughing.

Things at Eddie's house were going from bad to downright awful. He and his dad grumbled hellos. When Mr. Delaney asked Eddie to do something, Eddie did it grudgingly. He became more resentful with each passing day. Each time he saw his former teammates in the hallways, Eddie couldn't help but think if it wasn't for his dad, he could be with them. His friends were practicing for games and he was stuck in the house. It just wasn't fair.

Tayesha noticed how quiet Eddie was lately. She hoped that NEATE could think of something soon. She hated seeing her friend like this. In between swapping ideas on their essays, Tayesha thought of their plan and tried to work in some questions about his dad.

"What college did your dad go to?" she asked, out of the blue.

"What?" Eddie said and looked at his friend like she was crazy. "Who cares?"

"I just wanted to know," she replied. "I've been checking out colleges and universities. You know it's never too early."

"Shaw University."

"Oh, that's a historically Black college, right?" she said.

"Yeah. And?" Eddie said, visibly annoyed.

"Was he part of any campus groups? What job did he get when he finished school?" Tayesha probed, hoping to keep him going.

"Are you serious?" he said. "The last thing I want to do is sit here and talk about Floyd Delaney. I'd rather write a hundred essays."

"Sorry Eddie," she apologized and dropped the subject. That's probably all she'd be getting out of him. She hoped it would help—at least a little.

After Tayesha left, Eddie went upstairs. He sat in his room, headphones around his head, bopping to his favorite hip-hop CD. Mr. Delaney came home and spotted a full trash can in the kitchen. His mood instantly turned foul.

"Eddie!" he yelled.

There was no answer.

"Eddie!" he hollered again. Mr. Delaney's deep voice thundered through the house. He marched up the stairs, pushed open Eddie's door and entered a room adorned with posters of basketball stars. Clothes and shoes littered the floor.

"Didn't you hear me calling you?" Mr. Delaney said, his broad frame filling up the doorway. He examined the room with a sneer.

What now, Eddie thought. It was always something. He took off his headphones.

"Yes sir," he said.

"Why didn't you take out the garbage?" Mr. Delaney questioned.

"Huh?" Eddie said.

"The garbage," Mr. Delaney said. "It's still in the kitchen. What were you thinking?"

"I don't know," Eddie said. "I guess I forgot."

"You've been forgetting a lot of things lately," Mr. Delaney said. "You forget to study for language arts, forget to do your chores. You have no idea how lucky you have it."

Eddie knew he shouldn't say anything, just let his dad vent. But he was frustrated and tired. So he let his mouth get him in over his head.

"Why don't you tell me, dad?" he shot back. "How lucky am I? That's all I ever hear. I'm so blessed to have this or that. Daisey is so great and I'm so average. How do you think that feels?!"

"Boy, have you lost your mind," Mr. Delaney said and began to approach his son. "I know you're not talking to me that way."

Mrs. Delaney heard the commotion and rushed between them just in time.

"Floyd, Eddie, what in the world?" she said. "You all just need to stop this nonsense. It has been going on too long. Why don't the two of you end it now and make up?"

Eddie and his dad glared at each other. Neither moved an inch.

"You better tell that boy something," Mr. Delaney said before he stormed off. "He needs to take out the garbage. And I mean now. And clean that filthy room."

Mrs. Delaney didn't have to say a word. Eddie stood up and walked down the stairs. He knew better than to stomp. As he slammed the full trash bag on his shoulder and threw it into the can outside, he wondered if his dad would ever let up. Part of him felt bad that things had gotten so strained between them, but another side of him didn't care. He just wanted the freedom to be himself.

◆ CHAPTER SEVEN ◆

Naimah invited Tayesha and Liz to sleep over her house that Saturday. It was going to be part slumber party, part brainstorming session to compare notes about Mr. Delaney. Liz still had work to do. She had nosed around and come up empty. But mostly, she had been distracted by her own issues. She had never felt insecure about her singing. She had never envied anyone. Why did she feel so weird about Jasmine?

Liz and Jasmine had practiced a couple times after school. It was cool when it was just the two of them. They took turns singing and giving each other feedback. They talked about fashion and shared stories about auditions. But just when Liz started feeling better about Jasmine, something always came up to rub her the wrong way again.

Like one day, when Liz entered talent show practice, she saw Jasmine sitting in the middle of the two-story auditorium with a group of girls. She hadn't saved Liz a seat or anything. Liz, used to being in the mix, sat off to herself down front. It was a strange, uncomfortable feeling. She could hear the girls sweatin' Jasmine's style, her singing. No one seemed to notice Liz at all anymore.

"Liz," Jasmine called out when she spotted her.

"Liz!" Jasmine yelled as she tried to get her attention again. Finally, she walked down the aisle to where Liz sat alone. "Girl, I was calling you. Are you in outer space or something?"

Students sitting nearby laughed. Liz couldn't believe that Jasmine fronted her like that.

"No," Liz said, with major attitude. "I'm just concentrating on my song. I'm here to work."

Jasmine looked at Liz. Her smile faded and she walked away, hurt.

Liz felt bad but stayed right where she was. She peered at the stage and a black-and-gold banner emblazoned with the school motto "DuSable Pride" caught her eyes. It seemed that sign was meant for her. Liz wasn't pleased with what she had done. But she didn't know how to react. Couldn't Jasmine tell that she was in pain too?

That weekend, at the sleepover, Naimah and her friends claimed their spots in her cheery yellow room. One side of her space held bookshelves with neat rows of biographies and novels. The rest of Naimah's room was just as organized, bins for loose items, color-coordinated clothes hanging in her closet, CDs stacked neatly in a funky metal holder. Everything had a place. Tayesha, who brought a sleeping bag, crashed in a cozy spot near Naimah's globe and beanbag chair. Naimah pulled the trundle out from under her day bed for Liz. Once they got settled, it was time for business. Eddie was topic number one.

"So has anyone made any progress?" Naimah said after she sat pretzel-legged on the floor. "Let's compare what we know. I'll go first. My mom thinks Mr. Delaney might have been involved in politics even before he became a lawyer, maybe helping with a campaign."

"When I was studying with Eddie," Tayesha offered, "I learned a few things. His dad went to Shaw University, a historically Black college."

"Hmmm," Naimah said. "Anthony told me that his mom said Mr. Delaney is from Raleigh, North Carolina. He's also working on a lead that he doesn't want to reveal yet. Did you find out anything, Liz?"

"Nope, nada," she said, her mind someplace else.

"That doesn't give us much," Naimah said.

"Does anybody know how Eddie has been doing in Mr. Nelson's class?"

"As far as I know, he has been getting good scores on his quizzes and essays," Tayesha said. "I think he even got an A on the last one."

"Great," Naimah said. "We just have to keep it going. Well, unless you guys have anything else to add, I guess that's all we can do for now. What time is it?"

The girls looked at the clock and then at each other.

"Oh, no, we're missing videos," Naimah said before Tayesha could get it out.

They clicked on the TV right when an old-school classic came on—New Edition's "Candy Girl." Naimah and Tayesha giggled at the played-out fashions and moves. They couldn't believe that little baby-faced boy was Bobby Brown. Usually, Liz got in on the fun too. She would sing and dance in front of the TV. But this time she just sat there on the floor, in another world.

Naimah and Tayesha tried to get her to dance along with them, grabbing her hands to pull her up. Liz wouldn't budge, not even on her favorite part, the rap. After the song ended, her friends plopped next to her on the plush rug. When Liz passed up a video moment, something was definitely wrong.

"What's going on?" Naimah said. "I can't believe you didn't sing. That's your song."

"Don't even ask," Liz said, getting up and flopping onto Naimah's bed.

"Why? What's up?" Naimah said. She and Tayesha joined her.

"I don't know," Liz said. "Nothing, everything."

She was quiet for a while and then let it out.

"Is it just me? Or does it seem like Jasmine always tries to hog the spotlight?" she asked finally.

"I don't know," Naimah said, slowly. "I really haven't paid attention. What about you, Tay?"

"She seems nice to me," Tayesha responded. "But I don't know her all that well."

"Well, I've been watching," Liz said, "and it seems like she's always trying to get noticed."

"Hmmm," Naimah said, with a tease in her voice. "You aren't jealous, are you?"

"No, yes, I don't know," Liz said. "Why would I be? I know it's stupid. But I feel like I don't matter anymore. Liz is yesterday and Jasmine is now. I'm not even in high school yet and I'm already a has-been."

"No, you might be a bit of a drama queen," Naimah said and hugged her, "but definitely not washed up."

Liz laughed.

"Liz, you know that you can sing," Tayesha said. "I wish I had a voice like you."

"Think of all of the talent shows you've won," Naimah added. "Jasmine can't change that. She's new and just making friends. But you're the O.D., original diva of DuSable Junior High."

"Thanks guys," Liz said, smiling. "I don't know why I'm trippin'. I just never felt that I had to compete with anybody, for singing anyway. That was mine. But you're right. Jasmine is Jasmine and I'm me. There's enough school for both of us."

"That's right," Naimah said.

"You all are awesome," Liz said. "Group hug."

The girls stood up and embraced, giggling until they heard the notes of a Destiny's Child classic, "Independent Women."

"I know that isn't my song," Liz said.

She stood in the middle and struck a Beyoncé

pose. Naimah and Tayesha scrambled to either side to back her up. They shook their hips and grooved like they were opening at the Grammys.

The girlfriends crooned and threw their hands up in the air.

Everything was cool again.

◆ CHAPTER EIGHT ◆

That Monday after school, Anthony came home and spotted a bulging folder in the middle of the coffee table. When he got closer, he could see that his name was scrawled in his mom's writing on the yellow note stuck to the front. He sat down on the blue corduroy sofa and opened it up. Dozens of photocopies fell out. He scanned a few of them and saw that they were articles about Mr. Delaney. There was one that showcased his work with the NAACP, another that showed him with a group of his fraternity brothers walking for charity. He was quoted in law articles and in a couple that featured Mrs. Delaney's art. Then, Anthony began to see older articles from papers he didn't recognize. The pieces talked about civil rights, about young, Black people standing up to make a difference.

One article contained a photo of a boy who looked a lot like Eddie sitting at a lunch counter with a couple of other young, Black men. Angry White men leered at them from behind. Anthony read the caption. One name stuck out right away: Floyd Delaney. Anthony was so engrossed, he didn't hear the front door open.

"I see you found it," Ms. Young said, catching Anthony off guard.

"Wow, mom," he said. "These are deep. How did you get them?"

"I got some help from the folks in the research department," she said and smiled.

"Floyd is older than I am," Ms. Young told her son. "He grew up in the South. It was much a different time. You know about the civil rights movement and Jim Crow. Everything was separate. Movie theaters, lunch counters, even water fountains. Some people thought that Blacks were inferior to Whites. Do you understand?"

"Yeah, mom," he said. "I learned about that. But I didn't know that kids my age were part of it."

"Anthony, young people helped make the movement as powerful as it was," she said. "That's probably why Floyd is so hard on Eddie. Back in his day, young Blacks felt it was their duty to be the best. They had to prove that we could achieve as much as anyone else."

Anthony nodded his head.

"I bet Eddie doesn't know all of this," he said.

"Maybe you should go tell him," Ms. Young said.

Anthony nodded again and gave his mother a kiss of thanks.

"I will. But I gotta make a call first," he said.

Anthony called Tayesha and told her about the articles his mom found. He asked her to spread the word to the others. He didn't have time to call Naimah and Liz himself. He had to tell the most important person—Eddie. Anthony sped down Mary Street to the Delaneys'. He knocked on the wooden door. Mrs. Delaney answered.

"Hi," he said. "Is Eddie home?"

"No dear," she told him. "He's running some errands for me."

"Oh, could you tell him that I stopped by?" Anthony asked.

"Of course," Mrs. Delaney said.

Anthony walked back to his house with Eddie on his mind.

"I have to talk to him soon," Anthony said to himself.

Tuesday morning, Anthony got to the corner

where he always met his friends before school. He saw Eddie walking toward him.

Good, he thought. We'll have some time before everybody else arrives.

"Hey Eddie," he said. "I stopped by your house yesterday."

"Yeah, my mom told me," he said. "I'm sorry. I was just beat and didn't get a chance to get back to you."

"That's okay," Anthony said. "How are you doing?"

"Not that good," Eddie said. "My dad and I aren't talking. I said some things to him that I shouldn't. Everything is just a mess."

"I'm sorry, Eddie," Anthony said. "I know this has been hard on you. But I have something that might make you feel better. Could you come by my house after school for a few? I need to show you something."

"I don't know," Eddie said. "My folks are really on me. Our last argument was really bad. Now, they've tightened up even more. Is it something you can just tell me?"

"It won't take long," Anthony said. "You have to see this for yourself. I don't want to get into it now.

But you'll be glad you stopped by."

"Okay," Eddie said. "But I can't stay long."

Just then, they spotted the girls walking toward them. Tayesha had already told Liz and Naimah about the articles. They didn't let on to Eddie, but their smiles revealed their excitement. They hoped things would look up soon.

Liz knew she had something of her own to make right too. After homeroom, she waited for Jasmine.

"Can I talk to you for a minute?" she asked her.

"It's a free country," Jasmine said.

They stepped away from the between-class traffic.

"I just wanted to apologize for how I acted at practice the other day," Liz said. "I was really a jerk."

"Yeah, you were. But it's cool," Jasmine said. "Whatever."

"I think I should explain to you why I've been acting like this," Liz said. "Could you come to my house after school today?"

"There's no need, Liz," Jasmine said. "I said it's cool."

"I really want to explain something to you," Liz said. "Please say yes."

"Alright," Jasmine said. "I'll meet you on the stone steps."

She walked away quickly.

After school, Jasmine walked home with Liz. When the girls got to a ranch house with a large front porch, 513 Mary Street, they were there. Liz led Jasmine upstairs to her room. Posters of singers were pinned up everywhere in her cozy space: Alicia Keys, Mya, Christina Aguilera, Mariah Carey. Liz's talent show medals sat on a shelf like a collection of shining stars.

"So, what's up, Liz?" Jasmine asked and sat in a pink fru-fru chair.

"Girl, like I said, I'm sorry for how I acted," Liz said. "I was being petty. I don't know what got into me. I guess before you came, everybody was complimenting my voice. I was the diva. When people forgot about me and focused on you, I just got jealous. Stupid, huh?"

"No, it's not stupid," Jasmine said. "But you really hurt me, Liz. I told you how hard it was for me to make friends. You'll never know what it's like to move from city to city and start over everywhere you go. I'm always the new girl, always the one that gets tested and looked up and down. I thought this time was going to be different."

"I'm so sorry," Liz said. "I never thought about what you were feeling. I let the ugly, selfish side of me take over. I really want to make it up to you. Can you forgive me? Please."

"I don't know if I can trust you again," Jasmine said. "You just ditched me. That's not cool."

"Puhleeze," Liz pleaded again and stuck out her bottom lip to look really pathetic. She fluttered her eyelashes a few times to really ham it up.

Jasmine couldn't help but laugh.

"You're crazy," she said. "You're lucky I like you. Let's just start over."

"Hi, I'm Liz," Liz said. She extended her hand and smiled.

"I'm Jasmine," her friend said. She shook Liz's hand and grinned back. "You're nuts, you know that. I don't know why you were worried about my voice. When I heard you sing, I thought to myself, 'Wow, Jazz, you're going to have to raise your game.' You're way beyond me."

"Give me a break," Liz said. "I wish that I had

your range."

"I wish I had your power," Jasmine said.

"So are we still girls?" Liz said.

"Can Patti LaBelle hit a high note?" Jasmine said, smiling. They hugged.

"Can you believe the talent show is almost here? It's crazy," Liz said.

"I know," Jasmine said. "Do you want to practice a little?"

"Sure," Liz said. "Do you want to go first? Jazz? Jasmine?"

Jasmine just sat there, smiling.

"You know Liz, I just got an idea," she said. "Maybe we should sing something different for the talent show. Everyone is expecting us to go left, maybe it's time to go right. Are you up for it?"

"You talking to me?" Liz said. "Girlfriend, I'm ready for anything."

"What are you thinking?"

Jasmine shared her idea with Liz. Liz immediately nodded and smiled. She loved it. She couldn't wait until the show.

◆ CHAPTER NINE ◆

At Anthony's house, he and Eddie walked into the living room. The folder was still there on the black lacquer coffee table.

"This is what I wanted to show you," Anthony said. He opened up the folder.

"Newspaper articles?" Eddie said. "What's the big deal?"

He flipped through a couple of the articles before he noticed who they were about.

"A bunch of stories about my dad," Eddie said and slammed it shut. "Is this what was so important?"

"Wait," Anthony said. "I don't think you've seen all of them."

He pulled out some of the older articles and handed them to Eddie.

"Look, they're from the 1960s," Anthony offered.

"Okay, a bunch of *old* articles about my dad," Eddie remarked, uninterested.

Then he began to focus.

He saw the angry, White men and the Black students sitting fearlessly at the counter.

"Isn't that my dad?" he said, pointing to one of the young faces in the photo. "That looks like me."

"Yeah," Anthony said. "And there's more."

Eddie sat down and studied the photocopies.

"Where did you get these?" Eddie asked at last.

"Don't be mad," Anthony said. "But I asked my mom to print some stories about your dad. The girls and I hoped that we could find out something that would help you two get along."

Eddie looked at the articles again. Then he looked at Anthony with unspoken questions in his eyes.

"Can I take these with me?" Eddie asked his friend.

"Sure Eddie," Anthony responded.

"Thanks," Eddie said and set off for home clutching the folder.

Once he got inside, Eddie went right to his mom's studio in the attic.

"Hey honey," Mrs. Delaney greeted when she saw her son. "To what do I owe the pleasure of this visit?"

"Mom," he said. "What do you know about this?"

He held out the clipping of his dad at the lunch counter. Mrs. Delaney put down her brush and looked it over.

"Oh my goodness, where did you get this?" Mrs. Delaney asked him with a worried look on her face.

"Anthony gave this and a bunch of other articles to me," he said. "I knew that you and dad were involved with civil rights, but he never told me that he was part of a sit-in when he was young."

"You should talk to your dad," Eddie's mother said as she avoided her son's eyes.

"Can't you tell me about it?" Eddie asked.

"I just think it's something your father should tell you himself," she said.

Eddie headed to his room with the articles. He flopped his head down at the foot of the bed and propped his lanky legs against the head-board. Eddie stared at the photo of his dad at the lunch counter. Eddie wondered what that boy was like. He peered at his dad's steely eyes, the determined set of his mouth. His father had on his Sunday best. Even as a young man, his dad looked brave. Was he ever afraid?

Eddie had heard the stories of his dad's contribution to the movement his whole life. But to see those men crowded behind him, to see their glaring faces, that was something else. Looking at that group of men behind his dad made Eddie cringe. He could almost feel their hate.

He thought about how weird his mom reacted when he showed her the picture. She never shied from telling him anything. Why was she holding back now?

Eddie turned over in the bed, sank his head into one of his pillows and closed his eyes. He tried to imagine himself in his father's place. He felt the crush behind him, heard the ominous din of hostile voices. Eddie's heart beat quickened and he shuddered in his sleep. He woke with sweat beading on his face.

Eddie had to know what it was like. It wouldn't be easy. But he knew he had to talk to his dad.

Early the next morning, Eddie got up, grabbed the folder of articles and headed down to his father's office. Mr. Delaney was there getting a jump on his work. "Can I talk you for a minute, dad?"

"What do you need, Martin Edward?" Mr. Delaney said without looking up, in the business voice he used with his clients.

"I just want to talk," he said.

"Sit down," his father said.

They sat across from each other with the same serious expression. Eddie looked just like a young version of his dad.

"Why didn't you tell me about the lunch counter?" Eddie began.

"What?" Mr. Delaney said as his face took on a strange look. Eddie thought he saw fright in his father's eyes for a moment but knew he had to be wrong.

"I saw a photo of you at a lunch counter in Raleigh," he said. Eddie handed his dad the folder. Mr. Delaney flipped through the stories and pictures and frowned.

"That's old news." He shut the folder and slid it across the desk back to Eddie.

"Not to me," Eddie countered.

"I don't want to talk about it," Mr. Delaney said.

"Why not?" Eddie asked his father, who rapped his fingers impatiently on his desk.

"Since when do I answer to you, Martin?" he said. "I don't feel like talking about it. Leave it at that."

But Eddie kept going. When something mattered to him, he could be just as relentless as his father.

"Dad, I really want to hear about it," he said. "Please, it's important to me."

Mr. Delaney removed his glasses and slid his palm down his tired face.

"Eddie, you're really trying me today," he said. "I don't have time for this. I'm in the middle of working on a difficult case. You should be hitting the books yourself."

"Dad, I know that we haven't been getting along lately," Eddie said, softly. "I just thought . . ."

He looked at his dad's annoyed face and changed his mind.

"You know what? Forget about it," he said. "Forget I asked anything."

Eddie jumped up and strode to the door.

"Edward Martin," Mr. Delaney said sharply. Then, he toned down his voice. "Come back here and sit down, please."

Eddie quickly wiped the angry tears that had

welled up and turned to face his father. He sat back down.

"Why do you want to know?" Mr. Delaney asked him.

"I don't know," Eddie admitted. "When I saw that picture, I just wanted to know more about what happened."

"Alright Eddie," Mr. Delaney said and sighed. "You want to know. I'll tell you. But don't blame me if it's not what you want to hear."

"How old were you?" Eddie asked.

"About 14," Mr. Delaney said.

"That's just a year older than me," Eddie said. "Were you scared?"

"Yes son," Mr. Delaney said and gazed right into his son's brown eyes. "I was."

"So how did you get there?" Eddie asked.

A weary Mr. Delaney sighed again. He leaned back in his chair and let his mind take him back even further.

"I was a little older than you when the Student Nonviolent Coordinating Committee, or SNCC, as everyone called it, was staging nonviolent protests around North Carolina and other parts of the country," Eddie's father began.

"It was an organization founded by college students, but sometimes kids in high school like me participated in events too. Some students from Shaw University planned to demand service at the five and dime. They were going to sit-in at the Whites-only lunch counter like those guys did at Woolworth's in Greensboro. One of the college guys didn't show up so I filled in. No one knew how young I was until later."

"What happened then?" Eddie asked.

"Several White men surrounded us. I could feel their disgust and their hot breath on my neck. They started chanting: 'Niggers go home.' One whispered in my ear that he had seen me around and knew where I lived. I did my best to stand my ground like the others. I clasped my hands so that no one would see them tremble. I struck the strongest expression I could muster. Suddenly a flash blinded me. A photographer had snapped a picture. I was scared, confused. I could still feel the heat of their breath on my neck. Their threats kept ringing in my ears. It was just too much. I got up from that lunch counter and ran. I ran all the way home. When I got inside, I collapsed onto my bed and cried."

Eddie just sat there, stunned into silence. The wound gaping now, his father kept talking. Words poured out like rain.

"I was so ashamed. The other guys stayed and dealt with the consequences and I ran. I let them down, let down myself. I've regretted that every day of my life. That afternoon, alone in my room, with my heart so heavy I thought I would break, I promised myself that would be the last time I would run from anything. After high school, I went to Shaw and started learning about political science and the legal system. I knew right away that's how I wanted to make a difference. But none of the cases I've won can erase the humiliation of that day."

Eddie looked at his dad who seemed so vulnerable. He never imagined what his dad had been through, never thought to ask.

"I still feel bad about what I did," Mr. Delaney said. "I've kept it hidden from everyone because I was worried what people would think if they knew that the warrior for the disadvantaged had once been such a coward."

"Dad, you were so brave," Eddie said. "I can't imagine facing what you did. I'm so sorry that I've been fighting you so much."

"Thanks Eddie," Mr. Delaney said. "But I know what I was. I was a coward."

"Dad, haven't you always told me that real men make mistakes," he said. "That having courage means daring to try even if you might fail."

Mr. Delaney listened to his son, watched his face blaze with passion and realized that Eddie was growing up. He felt his soul lifting and his shoulders raising up.

"How did you get to be so smart?" Mr. Delaney asked.

"Maybe some from listening to you," Eddie said. "And maybe some from being me."

"So dad, is that why you've been so hard on me? Because you're still being hard on yourself for what you did back then?" he asked.

Mr. Delaney realized that he owed his son an apology.

"Son, when I'm wrong, I admit it," he said. "I'm never going to stop pushing you to be your best. But I've been holding you to an unfair standard. I apologize. When I was growing up, doing well in school wasn't enough. If you were Black and wanted to succeed, you had to be the best. Our collective achievements were greater than what any one of us could accomplish alone. All that hard work represented hope for future—just like you do. The day you were born, I looked at your tiny face—full of so much promise. I had so many dreams for you. I knew just what your name would be. Martin for Dr. King and Edward for my dad. Two strong men I admired. I wanted yours to be a life of power and purpose."

"It will, dad," Eddie said. "But I'm not you. I have to find my own way just like you did. But don't worry, you and mom raised me right. I'll be okay."

"I know Eddie," Mr. Delaney said. "I have been pretty hard on you. What do you say we call a truce?"

He stuck out his hand and Eddie clasped it tight.

"I'll tell you what," Mr. Delaney said, after a moment. "If you can raise your language arts grade by report card time, we'll talk about getting you back on the team."

"Really, dad?" Eddie said.

Eddie knew that he could do it. If his dad could deal with all of that madness in the '60s, Eddie could handle his challenge too.

◆ CHAPTER TEN ◆

Eddie dashed up his front steps to his house. He yelled for his mom when he got inside.

"What is it, honey?" Mrs. Delaney asked as she rushed to the living room.

"Plad-dow," he exclaimed, holding out his report card. "Your son has skills."

Mrs. Delaney looked over Eddie's grades.

"My, my, Eddie, I'm so proud of you," she said, grinning. "I know your dad will be too. We knew you could do it."

As soon as he heard the familiar turn in the lock, Eddie headed for the hallway.

"Hey Dad," Eddie said, with a sad voice and downcast eyes.

"Hey son," Mr. Delaney said, hanging up his coat. "What's wrong?"

"I might as well tell you now," Eddie said while he tapped his foot nervously. "Reports cards came in."

"Oh, Eddie, don't tell me," Mr. Delaney said

and headed for the sofa. "I better sit down for this one. Let me see."

He held out his hand and Eddie slowly extended the report card like it hurt him to give it up. Mr. Delaney sighed, a heaviness settling over his face as read down the sheet. Then, he saw the straight row of Bs.

"Why you . . ." Mr. Delaney said, looking up at Eddie. His eyes crinkled with delight as he realized the joke.

"Gotcha!" Eddie called out.

"Well, I have to say I'm impressed, Eddie," Mr. Delaney said. "You accomplished what you set out to do. I'm a man of my word. You held up your end of the deal. I'll hold up mine. If it's okay with your coach, it's fine with me. You can get back on the team."

"Alright," Eddie cheered. He did a victory dance in the living room, jamming like a running back who just scored a touchdown. Mr. Delaney's rich voice rumbled with laughter. Mrs. Delaney watched from the entrance to the room.

"Now, isn't this something to see," she said. "How about I take my men out to celebrate? What do you want to eat, Eddie?"

"Pizza," he answered triumphantly.

But before they went out, he had an errand to run.

"Is it okay if I go see Anthony for a minute first?" he asked.

"Sure," Mr. Delaney said. "We're on your time today."

Eddie jogged down the street and knocked on his friend's door. Anthony answered.

"Hey man," Anthony greeted.

"We did it," Eddie announced, before Anthony could say anything else. "I got all Bs. Thanks for your help. You the man."

Anthony grinned and corrected him. "No, Eddie, you did it," he said. "You the man."

The friends gripped in a handshake. That gesture said it all.

●●●●●

Days later, it was Liz and Jasmine's turn to sparkle. They could hardly contain their secret. The friends were so excited about the talent show. When the evening finally came, they had their plan together tight. Backstage, they helped each other get ready. They peeked out of the red velvet curtains and saw the throng of students with NEATE right in the middle of everyone.

The other acts seemed to rush by so quickly. Soon, it was time for Liz to go on. She stood near the curtain, waiting for her name to be called. She shook her arms and rolled her neck to relax. She was always nervous before a performance.

"Break a leg, Liz," Jasmine said, standing next to her.

"You too, girl," she said.

"Next, we'll have Liz Butler singing, 'Fallin,'" Mrs. Richardson, the music teacher announced.

Liz hurried out, whispered something to her and raced back behind the curtain.

Mrs. Richardson smiled. "Seems like we have a change of program tonight," she said. "Liz Butler and Jasmine King will be performing a duet."

The surprised crowd clapped as the music of Brandy & Monica's "The Boy is Mine" pumped through the auditorium. Tayesha looked at Naimah.

"Did you know?" she whispered.

"No, girl," she said.

Jasmine danced out first and Liz came right behind. Neither tried to outdo the other. Their voices complimented each other just right. Each riff Jasmine made, Liz matched. When Liz belted her part, Jasmine cooed a background line. Anthony, Tayesha, Eddie and Naimah got the party started by jumping to their feet. Everyone else started dancing too.

As Jasmine and Liz looked out at the crowd, they knew that it didn't even matter if they took first place in the talent show. They were having so much fun. They finished the song with one arm over the other and jammed their way out.

◆ CHAPTER ELEVEN ◆

Naimah, Liz, Anthony and Tayesha filed into DuSable Junior High's gymnasium for the last game of the season. A few weeks before, Eddie had convinced the coach to let him back on the team. Out of practice for so long, the former starter was rusty, and had been riding the bench ever since. But Eddie didn't sweat it. He was just happy to be back on the team. Plus he was going to high school next year. You bet he'd be ready.

At the start of the final game, the Bulldogs were leading. Eddie sat on the bench but grinned as though he were on the court. He was so proud of how far he had come. Then, in the last quarter, DuSable's rivals, the Globes, came to life. They seemed to get every shot they tried. It looked pretty bad for the home team. Eddie sat on the edge of his seat. C'mon guys, he thought, we can do this. Coach Hamilton shook his head as the Bulldogs missed a chance to tie the game.

The coach called his last time-out. Then, he turned to the bench and called to Eddie.

"Delaney," he said.

"Yes, coach," Eddie said.

"You're in," he said.

Eddie floated off the bench and into the group of teammates. He saw his friends pointing at him and cheering. His dad, who attended every game since Eddie was allowed back on the Bulldogs, held a thumbs-up sign. The coach laid out the play.

Eddie was psyched but he had to focus. He knew he could do it. He just had to concentrate. The final plays moved quickly. Eddie blocked a couple of shots. But the Bulldogs needed two points to tie and three to win. It looked like the end. Then, with just seconds left, Eddie had his chance to change the game. The ball landed in his hands. He was more than halfway down the court and three-pointers were his weakest shots. Eddie quieted the doubts, said a quick prayer, aimed and launched the ball toward the hoop with all his might. The crowd's eyes followed the ball as it neared the basket. It circled the metal hoop slowly then veered off onto the hardwood floor of the court. The crowd gasped and Eddie stood there in shock. His miss had brought the other team victory.

Eddie felt awful. He had begged the coach to

give him another chance and look what happened. How would he face his teammates, his friends?

Mr. Delaney was the first one onto the court.

"Way to go, son," he said and patted Eddie's shoulder good-naturedly. "I'm so proud of you."

"Proud of me?" Eddie said. "Why? I missed the basket. I lost the game."

"No son, you didn't lose," Mr. Delaney said. "You won in what really counts—doing your best."

Eddie had to smirk at his dad's pep talk. He sounded like an afterschool television special. But when Mr. Delaney stuck out his hand for their usual handshake, Eddie grasped it, pulled his father in close, and gave him a hug instead.

"Eddie, are you okay?"

Eddie recognized Anthony's voice and turned to find all of his friends crowding around him. Their faces were creased with worry.

"Yeah," he answered, as a smile slowly stretched across his face.

"Uhhh, well, what are you doing now?" Anthony asked, recovering from the surprise of his friend's answer. "Do you want to go to my house and hang out?"

Eddie glanced over and saw his father lingering nearby.

"I better pass this time," he said to his friends, pointing to where Mr. Delaney stood. "My pops is waiting for me."

He walked over to his dad and they left the gym side by side. At home, his father pulled the car into the garage. Eddie got out and advanced toward the door. Mr. Delaney picked up a basketball from a storage bin. Doink, doink.

"Not so fast," he called, dribbling the ball with a smile. "How about a rematch?"

Eddie paused for a moment and then grinned.

"Okay, you're on, old man. You better make sure you're up for it because I won't let you win this time," he teased.

"Oh, so, you let me win, youngster," Mr. Delaney said as he got his game face ready. "We'll see about that."

They stood head to head with a mixture of pride and happiness radiating from one to the other.

"Check," Eddie said and bounced the ball to his dad.

"Check," his father called back.

About the Author

Kelly Starling Lyons was born in Pittsburgh, PA and holds a B.A. in African-American Studies and M.S. in Magazine from Syracuse University. A features journalist, she has worked for *Ebony* magazine, *The News & Observer*, and the *Syracuse Herald-Journal*. Lyons lives in Raleigh, NC with her husband and newborn daughter. *NEATE™: Eddie's Ordeal* is her first published children's book.

Tell Us What You Think About **NEATE**™

Name _____

Address _____

City _____ State _____ Zip_____

Birthdate_____ Grade_____

Teacher's Name _____

School _____

Write down the title of this book. _____

_____

Who is your favorite character in this book? Do you know of anyone like Eddie? Or the other members of NEATE™?

_____

_____

What mysteries or cases would you like to see in future NEATE™ books?

_____

_____

How did you get your first copy of NEATE™? Parent? Gift? Teacher? Library? Friend? Other?

_____

Are you looking forward to the next title in this series? Why, or why not? _____

_____

Any other comments? _____

_____

Send your reply to:
NEATE™ c/o Just Us Books, Inc.
356 Glenwood Avenue, East Orange, NJ 07017
www.justusbooks.com

Please Visit Our Web Site and
Look for these other Just Us Books titles:

NEATE To the Rescue by Debbi Chocolate
NEATE: Elizabeth's Wish by Debbi Chocolate
NEATE: Anthony's Big Surprise by Wade Hudson

Dear Corinne, Tell Somebody! Love Annie
by Mari Evans

A Blessing in Disguise
by Eleanora E. Tate
Just An Overnight Guest
by Eleanora E. Tate

Kid Caramel: Private Investigator
Case of the Missing Ankh
Kid Caramel: The Werewolf of PS 40
Kid Caramel: Mess at Loch Ness
by Dwayne J. Ferguson

Reflections of a Black Cowboy: Cowboys
by Robert H. Miller
Reflections of a Black Cowboy: Buffalo Soldiers
by Robert H. Miller

Follow-Up Letters to Santa From Kids
Who Never Got a Response
by Tony Medina

www.justusbooks.com